MW00976944

silly Millies

Pleased to Eat You

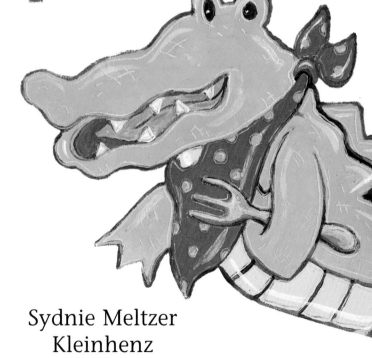

Sydnie Meltzer
Kleinhenz

Illustrated by
Beth Griffis Johnson

The Millbrook Press Brookfield, Connecticut

In loving memory of Ryan Cartwright (1993-2002), and for my other Big Little School students: Jakob Bressler, Taylor Clark, Rebecca Guilfoyle, Tyler Loving, and Samantha Russell.

—S.M.K.

For my two best guys, Nolden and Cooper

With love—B.G.J.

Reading Consultant: Lea M. McGee

Silly Millies and the Silly Millies logo are trademarks of The Millbrook Press, Inc.

Library of Congress Cataloging-in-Publication Data
Kleinhenz, Sydnie Meltzer.
Pleased to eat you / Sydnie Meltzer Kleinhenz.
p. cm. — (Silly Millies)
Summary: A child meets a carnivore, herbivore, and omnivore and finds out what each one eats.
ISBN 0-7613-2909-9 (lib. bdg.) — ISBN 0-7613-1827-5 (pbk.)
[1. Carnivores—Fiction. 2. Herbivores—Fiction. 3. Omnivores—Fiction. 4. Stories in rhyme.] I. Title. II. Series.
PZ8.3.K675Pl 2003   [E]—dc21   2002007499

Published by The Millbrook Press, Inc.
2 Old New Milford Road
Brookfield, Connecticut 06804
www.millbrookpress.com

Printed in the United States of America
5 4 3 2 1 (lib.)
5 4 3 2 1 (pbk.)

Oh!
Hello.

3

Pleased to meet you.

4

Pleased to eat you.

Pleased to eat me?

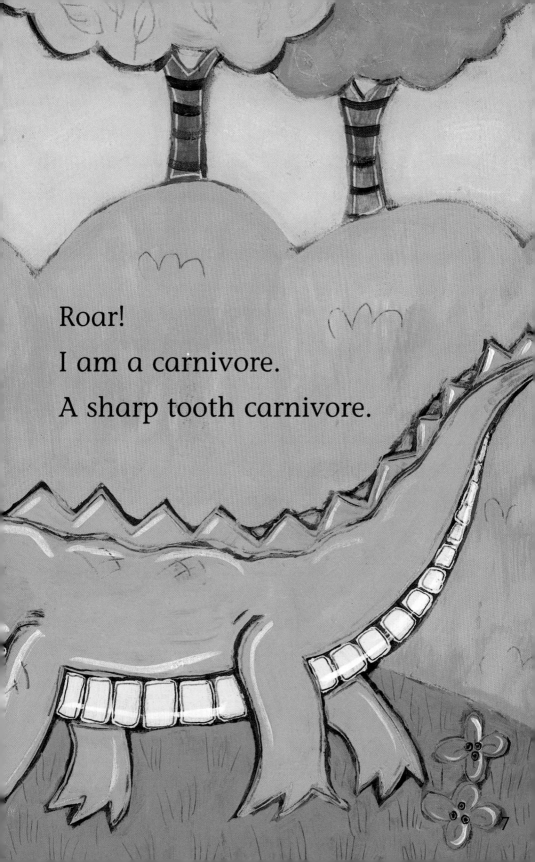

Roar!
I am a carnivore.
A sharp tooth carnivore.

When I meet you,
I want to eat you.

I will chomp and chew your head.
Then I will be fed.

But I will be dead!

I am a carnivore,
a sharp tooth carnivore,
and I just eat meat.

See you later, Alligator.

15

Oh!
Hello.

16

Pleased to meet you.
I won't eat you.

17

I am an herbivore,
a flat tooth herbivore.
I nibble and chew, but not on you!

I like plants,
but not the ants.

I am an herbivore,
a flat tooth herbivore,
and I do not eat meat.
I see some grass. May I pass?

Of course, Horse.

24

Oh!
Hello.

Pleased to meet you.

Pleased to eat you!

I am an omnivore . . .
and I eat *everything!*

Don't you dare, Bear!

Did You Know. . .

. . . that carnivores have pointy teeth to rip meat? Herbivores have flat teeth to grind plants. Omnivores have both kinds of teeth. What kind of teeth do you have?

. . . how scientists learned that grizzly bears in Yellowstone ate meat in the spring and plants in the fall? They looked at grizzly bear poop!

. . . that there are more herbivores in the world because there are more plant foods than meat foods?

. . . that young ants learn better when they eat healthy foods? This is true for children, too!

. . . how flamingoes and whales can be carnivores but have no teeth? They have long bony strips in their mouths that help them strain their food out of the water.

Dear Parents:

Congratulations! By sharing this book with your child, you are taking an important step in helping him or her become a good reader. *Pleased to Eat You* is perfect for the child who is beginning to read alone. Below are some ideas for making sure your child's reading experience is a positive one.

TIPS FOR READING

- First, read the book aloud to your child. Then, if your child is able to "sound out" the words, invite him or her to read to you. If your child is unsure about a word, you can help by asking, "What word do you think it might be?" or, "Does that make sense?" Point to the first letter or two of the word and ask your child to make that sound. If she or he is stumped, read the word slowly, pointing to each letter as you sound it out. Always provide lots of praise for the hard work your child is doing.
- If your child knows the words but is having trouble reading aloud, cut a plain white ruler-sized strip of paper to place under the line as your child reads. This will help your child keep track of his or her place.
- If your child is a beginning reader, have her or him read this book aloud to you. Reading and rereading is the best way to help any child become a successful reader.

TIPS FOR DISCUSSION

- Some things in this book are not real. An alligator would eat fish, but not fish fries. What else is not real? Can your child think of other funny foods?
- Humans are omnivores. What are some foods we eat that need flat teeth for grinding and sharp teeth for tearing?
- Think of some other animals and try to decide whether they are herbivores, carnivores, or omnivores.

Lea M McGee, Ed.D.
Professor, Literacy Education
University of Alabama